GRANDMOTHERS

ARE TO LOVE

Merry Christmas
Grandma,

Love,
Carol

GRANDMOTHERS
ARE TO LOVE

By Lois Wyse

Pictures by Martha Alexander

Parents' Magazine Press • New York

OTHER BOOKS BY LOIS WYSE

GRANDFATHERS ARE TO LOVE

TWO GUPPIES, A TURTLE AND AUNT EDNA

THE I-DON'T-WANT-TO-GO-TO-BED BOOK FOR BOYS

THE I-DON'T-WANT-TO-GO-TO-BED BOOK FOR GIRLS

To Cathy, Robert, and Wendy
who share the opinion that
"Grandmothers are to love."

This is a teeny tiny book
About somebody big who loves you.
Oh, there are a lot of people
Who love you:

The bakery lady
Who gives you a cookie,
And your uncle in Oscaloosa.
The next-door neighbor
With bangs loves you,
And so does the dog
Across the street.

There are two second cousins
Who love you,
And your teacher
Thinks you are a dear.
The milkman, the mailman,
And the bus driver love you.

And...oh yes...

So do your mother and father.

But this somebody who loves you
Looks a little like a mother,
Smiles a lot like a father,
And has two pictures of you
In her wallet.

This somebody who loves you
Makes good thick soup
And good thin cookies
And brings you sand from Florida.

This somebody who loves you
Takes you out to lunch
And invites you over to sleep.

This someone who loves you
Shortens your clothes and
Raised your parents.

This someone who loves you
Dries your tears,
Tells you stories,
And shows you which one
Is the Big Dipper.

This someone who loves you
Holds your hand
When you hop the puddles,
Holds you tight
When you feel sad,
And holds you up
To see the parade.

This someone who loves you is called
Mimi
Nana
Noo-noo
Gamma
Granny
or
Grandma.

But no matter what you call her,
She's your grandmother.

And if you have a granny
Aren't you the lucky one?
For grandmamas do many things
So grandbabies have fun.

When parents go away
Grandmamas run to do the sitting,
And if you need warm mittens,
Granny tends to the knitting.

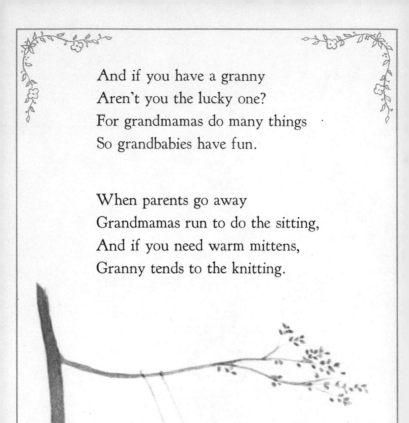

If you have some clothes
That you call your Sunday best,
Chances are it's Nana's gift
That makes you so well-dressed.

But the gifts of clothes and seashells
That grandmothers think of
Mean nothing next to your gift,
The priceless gift of love.

Why, Grandmother would rather have
The phone ring with your call
Than to have a real-live princess
Invite her to a ball.

Grandmother would rather have
A picture that you draw
Than a genuine Picasso
Hanging on her wall.

For the most precious jewel
Of Grandma
Is not a diamond or topaz,
But the precious little child
That her child now has.

You've a very special trust.
Remember this...please do,
The love of generations
Is handed down to you.

So if you have a grandma
Thank the Good Lord up above,
And give Grandmama hugs and kisses,
For Grandmothers are to love.